AF434710

STEEL AND BONE

Paul Duerr

thepaulseph Publishing

This novella is dedicated to everyone who has helped me become who I am. My mother, stepmother, brother, family, friends, and so many of my teachers.

CONTENTS

PROLOGUE

17 September 1862, Antietam, Maryland

"Fire!" the line officer shouted, followed by a disciplined crackle of gunshots down the line of battered infantry and dismounted cavalry. Explosions rocked the ground all around us, while bullets tore through the exposed heads of my friends. Our whole brigade was standing in line behind a snake-rail fence, parallel with the old Dunker Church. We had several batteries scattered around the battlefield that were dueling with the Federal artillery. The gunshots and explosions were constant, as was the shaking ground. We stood behind the fence, unable to move, simply trying to hold back the Federal onslaught with what ammunition we had left. We barely had any shoes, let alone working weapons to fight with.

Officers were trying to keep their men in line as the chaos kept unfurling. As one officer would shout an order, he would get his head blown off and had to be replaced with another, who would get his head blown off, and so on. I was covered in blood that wasn't mine, and the soil turned into piles of mushy, mutilated dead bodies. This had been happening for hours now. Their batteries have not stopped, and neither have ours. The arcs of soaring shells made the sky look as if it were about to rain, only not the pleasant kind. I would have given anything to run away from this nightmarish hellscape.

Eventually, the order reached us to fall back. What was left of our position was a series of craters, burning corpses, blood, entrails, heads, and various appendages. The Federals were welcome to it. After hours of bloody and brutal combat, the Army of Northern Virginia retreated back into northern Virginia, with no Federals in pursuit. We had lived to fight another day.

<u>Seven years later, The Calico Ranch, North Texas.</u>

I woke up every morning and did the same thing. Got out of bed at 5am, right when the rooster told me to. I put my boots, gloves, and hat on, walked outside to collect the eggs, tended to the cattle, milked the cows, and visited my wife's and son's graves. They were killed when some Comanche warriors raided our ranch a few years back. I swore to avenge them, and would do so in good time. After that, I fixed myself some dinner, and went back to sleep just to wake up and do it all over again the next day. It wasn't much, but it was honest work. I was 31 years old. A Civil War veteran, albeit for the wrong side, a widower, and a struggling farmhand. I had seen some real loss. My wife and son, countless friends during the war. I had to sell my ranch to old man Calico because I couldn't make ends meet. He robbed me, and damn near stole my land. Old Elijah Calico was the meanest son-of-a-bitch around. I heard stories when we moved out here saying that before the war, he was notorious, not only for being the local railroad magnate, but for having the slaves of his plantations beaten to death after they attempted to escape. Most people wouldn't kill their slaves because it was a poor business strategy, but he didn't care. He and his gang of thugs were bloodthirsty monsters. The bodies of those slaves looked more mangled than anything I ever saw on a battlefield.

It had been this way for three years now. Right after the surrender at Appomattox, we were paroled and allowed to carry on with our lives. I always credited Abe Lincoln for his "malice towards none, and charity for all" policies. He gave thousands of people second chances after they made terrible mistakes. Damn shame he was shot.

I met my wife out in California just after the war, and we married quickly after that. We were very similar in that we were both only children with no parents and seeking a new life. Not to mention, we were both from North Carolina. We had a little boy named Stuart, whose namesake was General Stuart, my old Corps commander, and we were very happy on our little ranch. It was almost too good to be true, and it was, when the Comanche came storming out of the fog early one morning. My wife and son were in the house, and I was in the barn. It churns my stomach thinking about what they did to them. I will never forgive myself for letting it happen to them.

I usually kept to myself and only went into town once a month to sell stock and buy feed and such. On the way back, I always had to stop at old man Calico's mansion just outside of town and drop off my rent to the guards just outside the gate. I had to be careful around them. They would sometimes raid my house and take silver and other items, claiming I shorted them on a previous rent, which wasn't true.

I led a hard and painful life, fraught with regret. I was longing for a change.

CHAPTER ONE

$$\blacklozenge \; \blacklozenge \; \blacklozenge$$

I woke up, as usual, to the sound of the roosters and the early morning sun leaking through a crack in the shades above my bed. I sat up, stretching my arms and yawning, before summoning the courage to stand. I had an outfit for the day folded on a chair next to my nightstand. I stumbled my way to the chair and equipped my blue jeans and tattered, sun-drained shirt. Yawning once again, I walked into the kitchen, fixing a pot of coffee to put on the hearth. Fumbling, I turned to notice the lack of heat radiating off it, realizing I had forgotten to actually light it. After mending my foolish ignorance, I managed a cup of coffee to start my day.

After enjoying the drink equivalent to dirt, I made my way out of the door and walked to the chicken coop in the early morning breeze.

"Good morning, ladies," I said while collecting the eggs from the half dozen hens. After collecting the eggs, I stored eight of them away in cold storage. The other two eggs I saved for myself, to be made into a delicious breakfast. I was planning to head into town this morning, as there were a dozen bottles of milk and four dozen eggs in cold storage that were slated for the market. It was perfect timing, as the person who delivers the ice is due to replace the blocks in there that melted away.

After tending to the cattle and loading up the wagon, I embarked on my monthly journey into the run-down town of Amberwater, Texas. The ride into town was fraught with sand, dust, and tumbleweeds. The stretch of road from the ranch into town was completely barren and run-down. It was a two-mile journey, which only took about 45 minutes given my mule was elderly and so was the wagon, but I made do.

Pulling in front of the general store, the usual crowd made their appearances. I knew virtually nobody in the town and kept to myself. The only person I ever talked to was the owner of the general store, Jeb.

"Morning, Jeb. A dozen bottles and four dozen eggs," I said, leaning on the counter and chewing on some tobacco.

"You got it. Here's your coin, I'll have your wagon unloaded." He placed the usual payment on the counter, five dollars.

"Thanks, partner." I collected the coins and

sat on the bench just outside while the wagon was being unloaded.

Sitting on the bench and chewing a new piece of tobacco, I noticed a commotion in the saloon across Main Street. There was a loud crash and a lot of yelling before a gentleman was hurled through the front window, narrowly missing a very out-of-place black Mustang, shattering the window and the frame. As he was attempting to stand up to defend himself, a tall bearded man, dressed in all black with gold lined accouterments, drew his ivory handled revolver and shot the drunk where he stood. He shot him right between the eyes and walked right back into the saloon. Before long, several men took the body away, as if it never happened.

"All set, Pierce. Have a safe trip back," Jeb said as he began to walk back into the store.

"Wait-what? What-just?" The door slammed behind him. I turned to see that the blinds had been closed in all the buildings on Main Street. The once bustling, yet run-down, Main Street was suddenly barren and abandoned within a blink of an eye. Literal tumbleweeds swept the street as the wind began to pick up. Dead silence filled the air until the only thing I was able to hear were my own footsteps on the creaking wood of the general store. I mounted my empty wagon, looking behind me to ensure I wasn't delusional, before cracking the leads and setting off, money in hand, for the Calico mansion.

The mansion itself was on a massive homestead. He made an incredible fortune off his railroad investments, being the majority shareholder for the North Texan Railroad Corporation and even having his own company, the "Calico Railroad Company." A large front porch had massive white pillars and a huge upstairs balcony, with gold lining each windowsill and all the handrails on the many staircases, coating the beautiful home. Green grass and trees adorned the inside of the walls and black iron gate, while dead trees and cactus lined the surrounding land that he did not own. He had lovely stables with no less than six amazing quarter horses. The place was built on the backs of hardworking slaves that he tortured and killed regularly, leaving their bodies for the vultures on the outskirts of his property. He thought the piles of bones were a nice decoration. A sick and despicable human being, he was.

Arriving at the main gate of the mansion a half-hour later, I noticed the same black Mustang from the saloon in the stable, as the guard at the main gate snapped his fingers and held out his hand with a mean look on his face. I handed him the cash, three dollars and fifty cents, and turned around to head home, as quick as I could. It was never a good idea to stay near that place for too long. He would shoot people if they stuck around for any longer than he liked. The crazy, delusional old man was pushing 85, and was still allowed to have his golden Henry rifle and sit on the massive upstairs balcony waiting to shoot anyone he didn't like the looks of. The sheriff stopped checking on him because of it. They were all too afraid to go near him, and they didn't think he was worth the trouble, at least, as long as they were on his payroll.

The ride back home was boring and tiring as usual, but it was most definitely an interesting trip into town. I had never seen anything like that in my entire life, and I was horrified to find out how and why it happened, and more importantly, if it could happen to me.

CHAPTER TWO

◆ ◆ ◆

I didn't get a wink of sleep that night. Most of it was spent laying in bed staring at the ceiling, occasionally peering out of a crack in the blinds to see if anyone was there. With every gust of wind my heart sank, thinking it was the man from the saloon. I even dug up my old Colt, holster, and sword from the war and kept it with me. Every passing minute felt like an eternity. I knew I couldn't go out for help, the Old Man bought off every sheriff within fifty miles of here. I suspect he even bought off the entire town of Amberwater. Luckily, after many hours of sleeplessness, the sun crept over the horizon and the roosters began their morning sermon.

Jumping out of bed, I readied myself just as I had done every day before, this time with a Colt strapped to my side. It definitely added an additional sense of security. Every task on the ranch was completed with haste and paranoia. Every time I walked from one area to another, I looked over my shoulder. With every errant noise I heard, from bushes rustling to the mule neighing, I put my hand on the holster. I was most likely overreacting, but it didn't hurt to be ready, just in case.

Next to the barn was the stable with a fenced in area for the cattle and my horse, Tanner. He was a trusty Morgan that I rode during the war, and kept all the way until now. I got him when he was just a young saddler, but now he's in his prime.

"Easy boy," I said, patting him on his mane.

Suddenly, the silence became deafening. The silence roused my suspicion and drove me to draw my pistol. Turning quickly, I noticed the door to my house open and swinging in the breeze. Colt in hand, I walked slowly towards the porch. Each step taken was cautiously planned to cause the least amount of noise. Each step closer resulted in trembling hands. The creaking door grew louder and louder as I made my way just outside the entrance. I summoned up my courage and ran inside the house, aiming a pistol at each corridor, clearing each room one at a time. Every time I opened a door, I felt a pulsing in my veins that I hadn't felt since the war. All four rooms were empty except for one. The final area I had to clear was the kitchen. I was waiting on an adjacent wall, listening to the shuffling in the kitchen. As I turned the corner, there was not a person in the house, but rather a small armadillo raiding my pantry. I chuckled to myself before opening the back door and letting the little guy out. As he ran away, I holstered my gun and turned around, freezing where I stood. The bandit standing in front of me had a gun drawn and was pointing it directly between my eyes.

"Don't mo-." He was cut off as he fell to the ground, revealing a tomahawk in the back of his skull, and, through the straight corridor leading to the kitchen, a gang of Comanche warriors standing in the center of the ranch. They were scalping another one of the bandits alive, his screams and pleas ignored. One of them was approaching the house to retrieve their tomahawk and claim the trophy of the other bandit they had slain.

I sprinted out the back and ran towards the stable, with nothing but the clothes on my back and pistol in my holster. I jumped the fence and mounted Tanner, who luckily already had his saddle on.

"Hyah, Hyah!" We jumped the fence and rode hard away from the ranch. Turning, I noticed about a dozen mounted Comanche launching fire arrows at my home, barn, and stables, while three of them rode towards me. I drew my pistol and kept riding away. For what felt like hours, we just kept riding before the Comanche finally gave up their pursuit, and we slowed to a halt, not knowing where I was. We were on a dirt path, which we followed until we saw an old wooden sign pointing left that said, "Thornridge, Five Miles."

CHAPTER THREE

◆ ◆ ◆

Arriving in the bustling town of Thornridge, Texas, completely exhausted, I noted the camaraderie, unlike anything in Amberwater. Kindness and compassion I had not seen since before the war - it was truly a sight to behold. People were helping one another with heavy baggage, smiles and handshakes were being exchanged, the streets were bustling, and the whistles from the rail yard could be heard. Looking to my left I saw the big sign on by the train station, "Calico Railroad Co." which completely dampened my hopeful mood. Those sons of bitches had a reach everywhere in the state. Between the Calico Gang and the Comanche, I knew I couldn't do it by myself, and I needed a crew of my own. I had let the graves of my family sit for too damn long without any retribution. When they were killed, I vowed to avenge them. I'd take down as many thugs necessary to make sure nobody ever has to deal with that gang or the Comanche ever again. And now, with no ranch to look after, I was free to do so.

I hitched Tanner in front of the local saloon

and made my way inside, wood creaking with each step I took. As soon as I opened the doors, the place gave off an immediate sense of division. The bar had a group of five or six loud and obnoxious fellas dressed in all black laughing and cheering, while the surrounding tables had people sitting over their drinks nursing them quietly and keeping to themselves or the people they were sitting with. I made my way to the bar.

"Barkeep." He turned. "Whiskey, please."

"You got it." He placed down a glass and poured it.

Taking the glass, I mistakenly bumped into one of the patrons sitting at the bar.

"Sorry there, friend," I said, apologetically.

"Who the hell do you think you are!" he yelled and got up from his seat. His friends joined him.

"Sorry, friend, it was an accident." I put the glass down and put my hands up.

The evidently drunk bar patron swung at me, hitting me in the face, knocking me to the ground.

"Now, sir, there is no need for violence," I said, wobbling back to my feet, wiping the blood from my lip.

"Talkin' pretty now, are we?" He swung again, but this time I blocked his arm and punched him clean between the eyes, breaking his nose and knocking him to the ground. Chaos ensued following his collapse. Patrons at the tables jumped and launched at the drunk's friends, who were fixing to kill me. I punched and blocked as men were throwing barstools and glasses all over the saloon. The barkeep was hiding under the bar as if it were a regular occurrence. Men were getting knocked down all around me. The people at the tables outnumbered the drunks at the bar, and the bar fight seemed to escalate. Broken glass and wood littered the floor as quickly as blood did. One of the patrons pushed the face of one of the drunks into the bar and kicked his head into it, knocking out his front teeth. I punched the hell out of two of them as the fight ground to a halt.

"Wow, that was a hell of a show!" said one of the patrons, bleeding from his forehead.

"Yes, sir, it was. Pierce Clayton, how do you do?" I said, shaking his hand, the rest of the patrons beating a hasty retreat.

"Pierce. Hank. Hank Edwards. I must say, Pierce, not every stranger who comes through here beats up some of Calico's folks. Damn impressive, you having the stones to stand up to them," he said, holding a towel to his forehead.

"So, they're a problem here too, huh?" I took a swig from a surviving bottle on the bar. "I came here escaping both the Comanche raiders and his gang. Both have been terrorizing around Amberwater."

"Damn shame. He controls everything from here to the border. Not everyone here is as keen to get rid of them, you were lucky coming into this bar. The folks in here were given an especially hard time by that group, including yours truly. I've been itching to get at those sons of bitches ever since they got here," he said, poking one of the unconscious gang members with his foot.

"Well, it just so happens I'm putting together a crew to take them down. You in?" I said, looking him in the eye and extending my hand.

"Well, shit," he shook my hand, "You don't have to ask me twice."

"To be honest, I wasn't planning on any of this, or for you to say yes that fast, haha."

"Welcome to the West. You never know what's gonna happen next."

CHAPTER FOUR

◆ ◆ ◆

We walked out of the saloon coated in blood and glass, trying to catch our breath.

"Follow me," he coughed, "I know a few guys who could help us." He walked across the street and four doors down and started knocking.

"Wake up assholes!" He yelled, banging on the door.

"What the hell do you - oh, hey." A rugged gentleman opened the door and greeted Hank.

"Hey yourself, this is Pierce, and we have a job for you fellas."

"Oh shit, how much you paying?" The gentleman's twin brother came running up to the other twin.

"Did somebody say money?"

"No," intervened Hank. "No pay, just killing Calicos."

"Well shit, why didn't you say so. Come on in fellas, coffee's hot."

"Thanks, fellas." We entered the modest home.

Walking into the house, my attention was

captured by a series of framed photographs displayed on the mantle of the fireplace. They were photographs of the twins in Federal uniforms taken just after the battle of Antietam, according to the labels below them.

"So you two were at Antietam?" I asked earnestly.

"Yes sir," one of them came over to me, "Corporal Lenny Starke, 6th Wisconsin Volunteer Infantry. My brother over there is Private Howie Starke of the same unit."

"No shit. Sergeant Pierce Clayton, 1st North Carolina Cavalry." We shook hands. "I see that photograph over there, says Dunker Church. Were you there?" I asked.

"Yep. Can't look at corn the same way after that bloodbath."

"I hear ya. My unit was detached, and we were on the fence at Dunker Church. Who knows, maybe seven years ago, we tried to kill each other."

"I believe it." There was a brief pause. "So, why this sudden bloodlust for those assholes? I mean, I get it, but why now?" Lenny asked as we took seats around the table in the living room.

"Well, I've been living under the thumb of them since some Comanche killed my wife and son in a raid on my ranch. Calico swept in, and has been taking advantage of me the past few years."

"Sorry to hear that, Pierce." uttered Hank.

"That's just the half of it. I ended up here because I witnessed some Calico bigwig kill someone in town, and I'm not exactly on their nice list. They sent a few fellas to my ranch, but the Comanche came back at the same time, killing them and torching my ranch. I hopped on my horse and just kept riding until I ended up here." There was a brief pause before Lenny intervened.

"Well, you came to the right folks. They killed our parents while we were out fighting during the war because they wouldn't pay." They all nodded in unison.

Hank broke the silence. "And they killed my wife and infant daughter too."

"They just outright killed them? No provocation?" I inquired earnestly.

"Yep. Cold-blooded murder," replied Hank.

"Well," I said, standing up, "then it looks like we have some work to do, fellas."

"Hell yeah," yelled Howie. "Come on Lenny, we have to go get our shit upstairs."

"Ok, we'll be back down in a minute," said Lenny, getting up from his chair.

A few moments later the twins came down the spiral staircase fully kitted out with a pair of revolvers on their hips, silver spurs, snake leather boots, frock coats, and matching black bowler caps.

"Looking sharp, gentlemen, let's go get us some mounts."

"Yes, sir, " Hank said, opening the door. "There's a stable just down the road with a few Morgans we can take. I know the guy," added Hank, "he won't mind, he owes me money."

"Perfect, come on fellas," I said, unhitching Tanner as we began walking down the street. We walked down to the stable, collecting three beautiful Morgans.

"Oh, perfect, they're already saddled," Lenny excitedly remarked. The three men mounted their new horses.

"Good," I said, mounting Tanner. "Let's ride!"

CHAPTER FIVE

◆ ◆ ◆

The newfound posse set out on the long road leading out of Thornridge. The burning Texan sun was directly above us. The air was dry, and the beads of sweat slowly dripping down my brow evaporated nearly instantly.

"Hey, Pierce," yelled Howie from the back, "where are we headed first?"

"Back to my ranch. There's some stuff there I want to get."

"I thought you said they burned down your ranch?" a confused Hank inquired.

"They did, but they didn't burn the cellar."

We carried on down the road for several long, grueling, and miserable hours until we finally returned to familiar territory with the sun beginning to set over the distant horizon. The farmhouse was engulfed in smoke and burning embers. The barn had also burned down, and the farm animals were wandering around the perimeter of the ranch. The cellar doors, however, still looked intact. I dismounted Tanner and walked towards the cellar doors, past the scalped and nude corpses of the men who tried to kill me before the raiders got here.

"You fellers stay sharp, I'll be up in a minute," I yelled, before disappearing in the bowels of my ruined home.

The clothes on my back were dirty, ragged, and drenched in sweat. I stripped myself of everything except my long johns and rummaged through one of the storage trunks, searching for new clothes. I stumbled upon my old war trunk and opened it to have a flood of memories seize my thoughts. My old cavalry boots, slouch hat, belt, holster, and great coat were there, and I made quick work of taking them out and putting them on. There was also a trunk of shirts, vests, and pants complete with my dad's old pocket watch. I fully dressed myself and walked out of the cellar.

"Goddamn Pierce, that is one hell of a look!" yelled Lenny from atop his horse. My cavalry boots were shiny and brown with golden spurs. My slouch hat was complete with the old CS emblem as well. My vest was matte black, my shirt was bright white with a red necktie. The great coat was gray, and the pocket watch added a nice golden accent to the black vest.

"It should look familiar to you boys, haha." There was a brief pause. "We're gonna hunker down here for the night, we'll be off first thing in the morning," I said, retrieving some blankets and firewood.

"So, Pierce." Hank walked over to me.

"Yes, Hank?"

"I know a guy about five miles east of here in Gold River who, I think, could be a big help. I think tomorrow morning we should take the trip east to meet him."

"That sounds perfect. I didn't know where we were going tomorrow anyway."

"Good, haha." Hank walked away to settle in for the night.

We all pitched in and made a decent bonfire in the middle of the property, surrounded by burned buildings. Our horses were hitched, our blankets were out, and we all sat around the campfire with baked beans and crackers. After I finished my delicious and elegant dinner, I lay back on my blanket, using my great coat as a blanket instead. I took off my hat and took one last look at stars that were sprinkled all over the vast Texan sky before putting the hat over my eyes and getting some well-deserved rest.

CHAPTER SIX

◆ ◆ ◆

I was awakened with a faint, "Good morning, Pierce," from Hank, as I removed the hat from my eyes and kept them closed as the burning sun was just rising.

"Good morning, Hank." I opened my eyes slowly, sat up and turned to Hank.

"Oh, shit." A man was sitting next to Hank with a gun pointed at him. The twins were still asleep as another stranger was searching through one of their bags.

"What do you fellas want?" I asked, as I found my holster empty when I reached for my gun.

"Well," the other stranger said, with my pistol in his holster, "just your stuff."

"Well, we need our stuff there, partner," I said while eyeing up the pistol in Lenny's holster just next to me.

"That's where you're wrong. Are you in charge here?" he asked as I fell silent. The one stranger by Hank then hit him over the head with the butt of his revolver as the second stranger asked the same question again.

"I guess you could say that," I responded, as I inched myself closer to Lenny.

"Ok, good." The second stranger finished looting our saddlebags and summoned his friend over. Hank was bleeding from the forehead on the ground as the two strangers arguing grew louder and louder. They were yelling about what to do with us. Before we let them decide, I jumped over to Lenny and grabbed his pistol, putting a lead bullet into the side of one of their skulls and emptying the rest of the cylinder into the other guy. The twins quickly jumped to their feet.

"What the shit!" they screamed in unison. I brought myself to my feet and put Lenny's pistol back into his holster.

"Christ, that was a close one. Howie, could you please check on Hank, I'm going to get our shit back."

I walked over to the bleeding corpses, one with a bullet in his skull and the other with five bullets in his chest, and collected my gun and all the personal items they took off of us. I returned respective items to their proper owners and repacked our saddlebags, including our blankets and such. Hank put a cloth on his head and carried on as normal.

"You'd think I'd get the hint and stop coming here," I said as I mounted Tanner, turned to the group and inquired, "Now, what do you say we ride out to Gold River?" They mounted their horses and followed me as we set off once again, this time for Gold River, a mere five-mile ride east.

Gold River is, suffice it to say, not the nicest place. It's only called Gold River because of the "gold" that was found in the river, which led to gangs and different dangerous types coming in and trying to take it all for themselves, only to find that it wasn't real gold, but fools gold. Pyrite. Nowadays, it's more of a layover place for travelers, which only has a few permanent residents in the center of the tiny village, and a saloon, which has rooms for rent. My wife, son, and I stayed there for a few nights on our way out here a few years ago. It was not a pleasant experience. A guy was thrown through the window downstairs while I was getting a haircut in the back, which strangely didn't seem to phase the barber.

We carried on down the road for another hour or so before finally arriving at the wooded town of Gold River. We crossed the bridge over the river itself and hitched our horses in front of the very large cabin-esque saloon at the center of the village. There was an incredible Arabian hitched out front as well. Hank walked up beside me.

"Let me go in first." He then walked past me and opened the door to the crowded bar. The twins and I followed. Hank led us to the dimly lit back room, where he greeted someone who looked oddly familiar.

"Jesse! How the hell are you?" Hank walked right up to him and shook his hand.

"Henry, good to see you!" the gentleman replied elegantly.

"Jesse, this is Pierce, that's Lenny and that one's Howie." The twins removed their hats as Hank introduced all of us. We shook his hand one after another.

"Fellas, how are you? Name's Jesse James. Have a seat."

CHAPTER SEVEN

◆ ◆ ◆

"You're Jesse James? The Bushwhacker outlaw Jesse James?" I asked as I sat down next to him. The twins bumped into each other when grabbing chairs, as they still had not blinked yet. Hank sat opposite us.

"Last time I checked, yep. What can I do for you gentlemen? The last time I saw Hank, it was to clear a bounty on his head." He smiled at the memory.

"Well, we have a problem with the Calicos-" He cut me off.

"Say no more. There's a wagon out back with all the weapons, explosives, and money you need. Feel free to take it and tell them Jesse sent you. Not only do I owe Hank a debt from saving my life a few years ago, those bastards have been interfering with my operations around these parts. You'd be doing me a favor." Silence filled the backroom.

"That would be- Thank you very much, Jesse." I shook his hand profusely.

"Anytime fellas, but I gotta get the fuck out of here. Remember, you don't know where to find me."

Before we could respond, he disappeared out of the door behind him.

"That was dramatic." Lenny chimed in.

"Oh good, you two are awake." I turned to Hank.

"Take them out back, get the wagon, and bring it to the front. I have some business with someone at the bar." I said walking through the crowd.

"This better not be any messy business!" he yelled at me. "Come on you idiots, we have to get the wagon." The three of them exited out the back.

I walked through the crowd to a woman at the bar who was sitting by herself. I approached her, and before I could say a word, she said,

"I heard you're out for the Calicos," her head hanging over her whiskey.

"Yeah, we are. You pretty much stared us down coming in here. Listen here-". She cut me off.

"I want in." She turned her head and revealed a scar on her left cheek.

"I remember you from Amberwater. When his son killed that guy in the street. That was my husband. Calico's son hit me after I refused to sleep with him, and my husband intervened. I've been wanting to get back at them and tear them apart. I want in."

"Ok. I can understand that. They killed my wife and son. We can use a passion for killing them like you have. Now, as long as you're in this group, you listen to us." She stood up to reveal a pair of golden colts strapped to her waist.

"Is that it?" she asked. "Well, this is gonna be fun."

We both walked out of the saloon to the wagon, which Hank and the twins brought out front. Hank was driving the wagon and the twins were atop their horses.

"You can ride with me or take Hank's horse." I said, turning to her.

"I brought my own." She was unhitching one of the most beautiful Arabian horses I had ever seen.

"Where'd you find her?" Howie asked, fixing his necktie. Lenny smacked him over the head, stating, "I'm six minutes older than you, she's mine." Lenny began fixing his necktie.

"She's none of ours. Leave her be. She's here for the Calicos, just like the rest of us." She looked at me with a sparkle in her eyes.

"And my name's Belle," she said from atop her wonderful Arabian.

"I'm Pierce. The one on the wagon is Hank,

those two idiots are Lenny and Howie."

"Hello, gentlemen. So? Where are we off to?" she asked.

"Well, we just so happen to have their home address and a lot of explosives."

Hank started laughing and cracked the whip to the wagon. We set off back towards Amberwater with explosives, and a well armed band of misfits with a bloodlust for the Calico gang.

CHAPTER EIGHT

◆ ◆ ◆

We rolled slowly into the town of Amberwater. As we approached, the streets became more and more empty as armed men came out of their positions to stop us. We finally reached the center of town when one of them approached us.

"Turn around and leave. This town is off limits to new folks."

"Good thing we ain't new." I pulled out my pistol and shot him in the face.

The Twins, Hank, and Belle all drew their guns and started blasting. I dismounted my horse and ran into the saloon and yelled,

"Everybody who doesn't want to fight, get the hell out!" A crowd of people swarmed around me, leaving two Calicos with fists raised. I shot one of them in the head as the other charged me. We brawled on the floor, punching, kicking, biting, and spitting before he got on top of me, and I was able to kick him off, up, and over me with both of my feet and through the window.

"That's the third goddamn window," I said to myself as I ran back outside to join the fighting, only to find that there was no fighting to join. The streets were littered with dead bodies as Hank, the Twins, and Belle were reloading their guns and smoking.

"What the hell, guys?"

"Well, you were in there for like, ten minutes," said Belle, lighting a cigar.

"Shit, it wasn't that long," I mumbled to myself, getting back on my horse.

"Alright then, let's go get the old man. Follow me."

I jumped back onto my horse as we hard rode at full speed down the road towards the Calico Mansion. Our five horses and wagon were stretched out along the road, moving as fast as we could, with the wagon at the rear. I slowed down to talk to Hank, who was still driving the wagon.

"There's gonna be a large rock next to the road just before we get to the house. We'll meet you up there."

"Ok," he said, as I rode off to catch up with the others.

Within ten minutes we were all waiting by the rock, watching Hank struggle to keep the horse moving. After another few minutes, he finally pulled up next to us.

"Ok, everyone unload the wagon," I said,

removing the largest crate labeled 'TNT'.

We started stacking arms, ammunition, and explosions next to the rock. Courtesy of the legend Jesse James, we had enough warfare supplies to destroy North Texas. We had a little over a hundred pounds of TNT, six shotguns, six lever-action Winchester rifles, a dozen Colt Navy revolvers, and enough ammunition to last a lifetime.

Belle uttered, "Jesus," as we stared into the pile of infinite glory.

"Well, what's the plan now, fellas?" she asked.

"Alright, here's what we're going to do…" I then devised a plan over the course of a few minutes. After explaining what we were going to do, everyone split into their various positions. I sat behind the rock and waited for the signal to commence the distraction. Suddenly, a bird call broke the silence and I jumped into the wagon, loaded with covered explosives. I took the wagon onto the main road and drove it right up to the main gates, noticing a glimmering light on the hill behind the mansion. The guard approached me,

"Delivery for Mr. Elijah Calico?" he asked.

"Yes." I responded.

"Good. You're late, they've been expecting you. Go on in."

"Thank you." I cracked the whip and parked at the center of the compound and dismounted. A guard approached me with his gun out.

"Don't just leave that here, park it over there."

"I was told to leave it here." I stood my ground as four more guards approached.

"What's the problem here?" another one asked.

"You see-" I ran in the opposite direction as two more guards jumped on the back of the wagon to investigate. Seconds later, while I was taking cover, a shot rang out aimed for the explosives in the back. As the bullet hit, the shockwave knocked over the shed I was leaning against, knocking me down. Body parts and blood rained from the skies as black smoke, gunshots, and screaming filled the air. The twins and Hank tore in on their horses with shotguns as Belle was sharpshooting from the hill. I drew my pistol and joined the action, blasting everyone and leaning against the Twins and Hank, who had just dismounted and were taking cover behind the marble fountain in the middle of the compound. A massive firefight engulfed the compound, with dozens of armed guards getting torn apart all around us. After several minutes of blasting and reloading, the gunfire finally ceased.

"Holy shit!" I yelled as I took off my hat and holstered my gun, "That was a hell of a scrap, wasn't it? We should check the house, too."

"Ok. Just give me a second to catch my breath." Lenny muttered under his breath.

"BELLE! YOU CAN COME DOWN NOW!" Howie screamed at the top of his lungs.

The five of us had our guns out as we cleared the house out one by one. We found the entire four-story mansion empty. Not only from people, but from everything. There were no horses in the stable, no wagons, no furniture, nothing at all. Hank came up to me with a note and blood on his hands.

"I found this on a body." I took the note which read,

The last shipment just arrived on the train. We are waiting at Thornridge for the Old Man and Joshua. Once they get here, you can spring the trap.

-Butch.

I didn't know who Butch was, why there was a trap, or who it was for.

"Does this make any sense to you?" I asked Hank,

"No. There are no other rival gangs around here. The only people I can think of are the Comanche."

Suddenly, it hit me. "They have a village near here, right? And they've been raiding all around here and interfering with Calico operations? Perfect." I said.

"What?" he asked.

"We're going to visit the Comanche." I walked out of the front door of the mansion.

"Hey Pierce, we got a live one!" Lenny said, dragging over a wounded guard.

"Please, I hate it here-" he pleaded as I shot him between the eyes.

"Tell them the Clayton Gang sent you," I said without breaking stride.

"The Clayton Gang?" Belle asked. "I like it."

We cleaned ourselves off and reloaded our guns. The newly christened Clayton Gang mounted our horses and rode out of the gates while torching the mansion and leaving a burning path of destruction in our wake.

CHAPTER NINE

◆ ◆ ◆

The Comanche village was a mile off the road into the woods. Belle said she knew where it was because her husband used to trade with them back in the day. We rode over Amberwater Creek and through the dense woods until we finally reached the village. It was absolutely immense and incredibly well hidden for its size. There were dozens of lodges and people ready to greet us as we rode into their village. It was almost as if they were celebrating. Belle hopped off her horse and started speaking to them in their native language, while the rest of us dismounted and stared in utter confusion as we were swarmed by a massive crowd of them. They tried giving us gifts, holding and shaking our hands, hugging us, it was as if we just won a war. Belle broke through the crowd to talk to us.

"They are celebrating because we burned down Calico's mansion."

"So, the enemy of our enemy is our friend?" I asked.

"It's looking that way, Pierce. I told them everything, and the Chief wants to meet with you."

She took my hand and led me to the Chief's lodge. We were being showered on with beads and corn as we passed through the ecstatic crowd of Natives, straight into the chief's modest lodge covered in pelts and antlers. Belle and the Chief exchanged a Comanche greeting, and he gestured for us to sit. We looked at each other for what felt like an extended period of time before he broke the silence.

"My name is Chief Cuhtz, or Buffalo. I am told you are Pierce Clayton. I understand that it is your aim to destroy Calico."

"Yes, sir, it is." I replied nervously.

"We have been in conflict with his people for years," he said, "They would disguise themselves as our people and raid innocent homesteads and ruin our name. We are prepared to give you anything you need to take on this menace. My son, Tseena, will join you. His name is Wolf in your language."

"Thank you very much, Chief Buffalo," I replied.

"Of course. Now go, you must start on your journey to destroy this menace."

"Very well. Good day sir." We left the tent as Belle and the Chief hugged one another.

Wolf brought his horse over to ours and looked ready to go.

"Hello, Wolf. My name is Pierce." I extended my hand to shake his.

"I have heard of you. I am to join you on your quest to destroy the Calico."

"Yes, you are. Alright, everybody, mount up."

We mounted our horses as a roaring crowd cheered us out of the village. We set off once again for the bustling town of Thornridge. I was still struggling to deal with the reality that the Comanche may not have been the ones who burned my ranch and killed my wife and son. This only emboldened my desire to mutilate the Calico family one at a time. My mission was to bring them down at all costs, not only for myself, but for all the lives they destroyed. Wolf rode up next to me.

"I like your group. The fat one smells funny." He then rode off.

Hank yelled from the back, "Hey, I heard that! What the hell?"

CHAPTER TEN

◆ ◆ ◆

We had traveled off the beaten path to follow the railroad tracks into Thornridge. The particular line we were following ran from Chicago through Dallas and all the way to San Francisco. After a few hours, and as the black cloud of smoke over the old Calico mansion grew distant, we finally made it into the town to find no train in the rail yard. We had missed the Old Man's train by hours. Hank rode beside me as we carried on through the town.

"We shouldn't stay here. We should get through here as quickly as possible and go to the next town to see if we can get clues as to their destination."

"Ok," I replied, "What's the next town?"

"I believe, King City."

"Perfect. We'll ride there, ask around, and spend the night."

"Sounds like a plan. Let's go fellas!" he said as I rode to the front with the gang behind me.

We tore through town as quickly as possible as to not be recognized from our previous encounter here. King City was ten miles from Thornridge, and there was nothing but barren desert and railroad tracks in between. The unrelenting and burning Texan sun was squarely above us as our horses huffed and puffed their way through the dust and cacti. Those of us who chose all black as our outfit of choice were having second thoughts. Halfway through the trip, I finished the last sip of water in my canteen, and everybody else was dangerously low. Thankfully, Wolf had brought enough water to last days in the desert and shared with us while insulting us in Comanche. Belle later told me it roughly translated to 'complete and utter morons.' Regardless, we and our horses were well watered, and we made it to King City.

This was my first time in these parts. None of us had been through here before except Hank, and he neglected to mention that it was a barren, rundown wasteland. The only things that looked halfway decent were the saloon and the railway station. Come to think of it, I don't think you need much more in a western town. There were exactly six hitching posts in front of the saloon, so we took up every single one and went inside.

The inside of the saloon looked surprisingly decent. There was liquor on the shelf worth more than a bucket of warm spit, and the barstools looked somewhat stable. Everyone, except me, took a seat at the bar and ordered drinks, while I excused myself and made my way to a poker table in the corner that had one seat open.

"Mind if I join you fellas?" I asked the honest looking gentlemen.

"It's a free country," one of them replied as he spit into a spittoon. They dealt the cards, two per person, and they put down the big blind and small blind.

"Hope you like two card poker," another one of the poker players asked.

"I most definitely do." I looked down at my hand to see a seven and a two, unsuited. I looked around the table and read my competition. I knew I had this in the bag, but also took note of the revolvers strapped to their hips.

We went around the table and put down our money before the dealer put down the first three cards. It was a five, a six, and an ace. One person folded and one person raised. I called, and the next card was put down. It was a four. I raised because I was dumb enough to chase a straight, and another person folded. The only other player that hadn't folded was the dealer. He called and put down the last card, a three. We both checked and revealed our hands. I had a seven high straight, and he had three of a kind aces. After an inappropriate amount of cussing and swearing, I was the only one left at the table. There were twenty dollars in front of me, which I brought to the barkeep.

"Three rooms and drinks on me," I said, as the gang cheered and poured me a shot of bourbon.

The last thing I remembered from that night was Wolf carrying my drunken hide upstairs to my room. The twins shared a room, Hank shared with Wolf, I shared with Belle. After he placed me on the bed across from Belle, I completely blacked out. I also may or may not have urinated on a plant before passing out. Regardless, that night was most definitely a much-needed rest from our current mission.

CHAPTER ELEVEN

◆ ◆ ◆

Waking up from my drunken slumber rendered me immobile. I laid in bed for most of the morning before Belle dumped cold water over my head, causing me to launch straight up into the coffee she was handing me, almost as if it were a perfectly executed ballet of morning shenanigans. I sipped the coffee and asked Belle,

"What the hell happened last night?"

"You got drunk, pissed in that plant, and fell asleep. Now come on, everyone is waiting for us," she replied as she walked out the door.

"Ok." After stretching and getting fully dressed, I made my way downstairs to the rest of the gang. I approached Hank first.

"I think we should ask around here before moving on to the next town."

"Most people here are drunk or dead," he replied.

"Ok, what's the next town?" I asked.

"Plainlanding. The rail goes through there and there's a fair-sized farming community there. Good, hard workers."

"Sounds good. We'll follow the tracks down there," I said, as we mounted our respective horses yet again and set off for the quaint town of Plainlanding.

As opposed to the harsh deserts between the previous towns, the landscape began to alter with every mile we traveled. We started traveling through barren plains, scorching deserts, then through dense forests, and now rolling hills. We had come across a variety of wildlife, from bears to buffalo, scorpions to snakes. We moved through thick marshes and crystal clear waters and experienced everything from arson and gunfights, to poker and drinking all during our memorable pilgrimage.

Plainlanding was situated cushioned between three hills with the railway station towering above it. As we approached it and came up over the hill, the view revealed countless miles of farmland, uninterrupted for miles except for the railroad running through it. After leveling out on top of one of the hills, we began our descent down the road into town and rolled through the streets. None of us, not even Hank, knew where this town stood as far as being friendly with the Calico's, so all we could do was to be blunt and ask around. We rode next to someone on the sidewalk.

"Hey there, have you ever heard the name Calico before, fella?"

"Piss off," he mumbled, as he took a swing from a hidden flask and tumbled into the saloon.

"That was uninformative," I said to Lenny. "Let's ask that guy." We rode up to a towering black gentleman.

"Hello sir, have you ever heard the name Calico before?" I asked.

"I hate that son of a bitch. He can rot in hell," he replied without skipping a beat.

"Perfect," I said. "We just so happen to be trying to bring down him, his family, an-"

"Can I join you?" He jumped onto the horse he had just hitched, "It's perfect timing too, his train just passed through here, name on the sides and all."

"Shit! We gotta go. Yes, you can come with us. Do you happen to know where he's headed?" I asked, gripping the reins and preparing to crack them.

"Yeah, he's high tailing to Dallas. His headquarters is there." Without even thinking, I cracked the whip and tore down the road, the rest of the gang behind me. Within a minute, we were outside of Plainlanding, following the tracks all the way to Dallas. It was noon and the ride was thirty miles, but I was determined, and so was the gang.

CHAPTER TWELVE

◆ ◆ ◆

At full gallop, we made the ride to Dallas in two hours, just as his train was gearing up to leave the station. His guards were waiting at the rear and began firing at us as soon as we were in range. My wartime cavalry experience took over as I drew my pistol and began evasive maneuvers and we, and the train, both began speeding up. The train was moving fast, and only my horse and Belle's were able to keep up. The guards and I took turns firing at one another for a few minutes, but then Belle swooped in from the right and killed both of them. We both sped up alongside the train until we came across a flat railroad car, me on one side, Belle on the other. I raised slowly out of the saddle as the horse and train were moving full speed ahead. My life flashed before my eyes as I took the leap of faith from the saddlebag to the train with my eyes closed. When I opened them, Belle was there with her hand out to help me up. I took it, got up to my feet, and drew my gun.

People were coming from the front and the rear. We moved as quickly and efficiently as possible towards the engine, blowing people down. We passed through the Old Man's private car, which he was not in. It only had guards and his incredibly ornate decor lining the walls and furniture. After picking off the guards, we took a few minutes to search his desk, safe, and the dozens of other compartments, only to find everything completely empty. We kept moving forward through the train, passing through the space between the cars ever so carefully.

We finally made it to the coal car, which we would have to scale in order to get to the engine. I climbed the stepladder first, Belle followed. We were both atop of the coal car aboard a moving locomotive, the coal shifting with every small movement. Our steps were timed so that she walked where I did. Suddenly, the train turned down a fork in the tracks. The bump sent Belle over the side, with her hanging on for dear life.

"Hold on!" I yelled as I dove towards her, grabbing her hands.

"What the fuck do you think I'm doing!" she yelled. I hoisted her from the side and set her down safely on the ledge between the coal car and the engine.

The precarious gambit paid off as we reached the other side mostly unscathed. Guns drawn, we opened the door to the engine, only to find the car empty. We searched around and found the instruments completely out of commission, rendering the train rogue and unstoppable. The brake lever was broken clean off, and Belle looked out the window to see ahead and screamed.

"Pierce! Look!"

I looked out the side to see an incomplete bridge over a valley. The train was the trap. Without a second thought, I ran over to her side, grabbed her, and jumped, landing full force on my back with her on top, rendering me unconscious. The train careened onto the bridge and hurled towards the bottom of the ravine, one car at a time, in a fireball of wreckage and flames.

CHAPTER THIRTEEN

◆ ◆ ◆

"Pierce..." a voice said that faded into darkness.

"Pierce....we need to go..." The same voice again. A few seconds went by before I was violently awakened with a slap across the face from an angry Belle.

"Get up hillbilly, the gang's waiting," she said, mounting her horse.

"Jesus Christ, you are the queen of rude awakenings," I said, stumbling to my feet.

"That's what you keep me around for. Come on, we have to get back to Dallas."

"Ok." I stood unsteadily on my feet and mounted Tanner. "Let's go."

A dark rain cloud covered the sky above us between the ravine and Dallas. We rode at full gallop as a torrent of rain pelted the ground and landscape surrounding us. Thunder was rumbling in the distance and lighting was striking frequently. One bolt of lightning struck a tree next to us, igniting it and launching wooden shards at us, almost as if it were shrapnel from Federal artillery during the war.

Regardless, we made haste into Dallas just in time.

"Pierce! What the hell happened?" Hank asked as he helped me off my horse.

"A fucking trap. The train was on an unfinished track straight into a ravine."

"Shit." He began pacing, his signature move when he's thinking.

Suddenly, a gunshot rang out and Lenny tackled me, "Fuckin' shit!" I yelled as he dove to the ground with me. The next few minutes were a complete blur for me. It was almost impossible to comprehend. Standing in the rain was the man we picked up in Plainlanding, pointing his gun at me. He revealed himself as a Calico agent sent to assassinate me in case the train plot failed. Within a split second, as he cocked his gun for another shot, an arrow fresh from the bow of Wolf hit the man dead between the eyes, leaving a gnarly sight of mangled flesh as his corpse collapsed in a heap onto the ground.

I turned to Lenny, laying next to me. "That was a close one." I noticed a puddle of watered-down blood seeping into the mud coming out of his chest. He wasn't breathing. His lifeless body was next to me in the mud and blood as the rain came down harder and harder. Howie dropped to his knees in front of us, sobbing and screaming. He then stood up with a knife and made his way over to the corpse of the man who killed his brother. Hank went over to him and embraced him, holding him down as he cried.

"Why!" he shouted and went on to cry for several minutes. I was nearly overcome with shock, but Belle knocked some sense into me. That man saved my life. I walked over to the pair, who were attempting to console one another.

"No matter what, we will make sure these bastards pay for what they did. I will fight them until my last dying breath. I will squeeze that geezer's neck until his last puff of air is red. But I can't do it without you. Are you with us?"

Howie took a moment to compose himself before responding with, "Fuck yes."

CHAPTER FOURTEEN

◆ ◆ ◆

We covered the body and left him to lay to rest after Wolf said some Comanche prayers. The rain finally let up, and we were in the middle of the Dallas Railway Station.

"Fellas, we've been gallivanting all over North Texas and have come across nothing but traps and meaningless death searching for this son of a bitch," I said. "I think it's about time we made him come to us."

"How do you plan on doing that?" Hank asked.

"We'll break up into pairs and recruit like madmen. We'll put together a proper gang. We will raid and pillage everything with the Calico name on it until he has to come out and face us. We need to take a score, so we can get enough seed money to have a few dozen people on payroll. And I see it right over there." I pointed to a sign that said 'Calico Mining Co.' on the other side of Dallas, in the outskirts.

"So, you're planning on robbing a goldmine in order to exponentially grow your gang and draw out one of the most notorious robber barons in the west?" Hank asked.

"Yep."

He looked shocked. After a brief moment, all he said was, "Alright."

"Wolf, you should set off back to your village and recruit any young warriors you think could help. Hank and Howie, you take everything east of Dallas as far as Old Grove. Belle and I will head back towards Amberwater and see what we can do back west. When you recruit, tell them they start getting paid after the first job. Make sure they know it isn't a one-off. When they are recruited, they work for the Clayton Gang. We will meet back here one week from now. That's when we will take that mine," I said as I mounted my horse.

"Ok, works for me. Good luck fellas." Hank shook mine and Wolf's hand as he and Howie mounted their horses and set off. Wolf gave me one of his unnerving glances as he, too, set off.

Belle turned to me and said, "Well, it looks like it's just you and me."

"That it is. I never thanked you for saving my life."

"Don't thank me, kiss me." She leaned in and kissed me. I pulled back quickly and said,

"Though I did save yours too-" She shut me up in her own special way again.

We set off once again for the town of Amberwater, searching for more members for our merry band.

CHAPTER FIFTEEN

◆ ◆ ◆

We rode for five hours, making it as far as the quaint village of El Diablo. The name is misleading, as it is actually named 'The Devil' for its population of horned lizards, oddly enough. Some Spanish conquistadors a few hundred years ago must've thought them to be Devil's creatures. The town, as I remember it, had a central saloon with two streets on either side of it, making the establishment something of a capital for the town's two hundred or so miners. The silver mine in the hills just beyond the town is one of the few mines around these parts that do not have the Calico name stamped on them, which was promising. Belle and I rode to the saloon and hitched our horses in front.

"For such a beautiful horse, you must have a hell of a name for her." I turned to ask her as she dismounted.

"I do. It's Rose. Beautiful from far, but a real prick if you piss her off."

"I expected something along those lines. Let's head inside."

The saloon was actually quite nice. The bar

was polished mahogany and there was decent liquor on the shelves. The upholstery was decadent and the ambience was cheerful. People were all around us having a grand old time. We approached the barkeep to ask an important question.

"We're here to do recruiting for a job. Is it ok if we take that back table?"

"No problem. It's a dollar for the night," he said. I put down six dollars on the counter.

"Thank you, we'll take that and a room."

"You got it, boss."

We made our way over to the table through the bustling crowd and set up shop. Belle turned to me as she was placing down a sign-up sheet and asked,

"How do we know this place isn't Calico friendly?" I didn't say a word. I pointed to the dartboard, which had a picture of Elijah Calico's face on it. She glanced at it, and promptly sat down to finish working on the information sheets we were going to distribute. Before long, people got word as to why we were here and came signing up in droves. There was a group of about eight people around us. I stood up and said,

"Make an orderly line. Once you make your mark, you can take this information sheet." Belle pulled out a small stack she had been working on and put it next to the roster sheet containing all the details of the job. "We ride tomorrow morning."

And so, as each new recruit made their mark and signed on with the gang, we made good progress to bring down that brigand Calico. It was about time we gave him a taste of his own medicine. When the clock struck midnight, we had fifteen people signed on the roster, and all of our information sheets gone. We gathered our belongings, placing them in one of the trunks, and made our way upstairs for some much-needed rest before we headed to the next town. I went straight to bed, but Belle insisted on making more information sheets before joining me.

CHAPTER SIXTEEN

◆ ◆ ◆

The sun rose, the light creeping through the blinds, growing brighter and brighter. Belle was already awake, getting dressed and packing our trunks. I rolled out of bed, dressed, and helped her pack. Once we finished, we made our way downstairs and loaded up the horses and hopped on. With our recruits in tow, we made our way to the next town, Boone. Our party of seventeen kicked up enough dust on the way to town that a new hill was beginning to form behind us. It was a relatively short trip. However, it was ill-met when we arrived. A few men with guns stopped us on the bridge into Boone.

"Turn back. Strangers ain't welcome here," one guard said sternly.

"Well, last time I checked, it's a free country."

"Just following orders, partner. Turn around and head away." He cocked his gun.

I put my hand on my holster. "I don't think I will. Who's orders?"

"Joshua Calico. Now get the fuck out of here."

Joshua. I knew that name from somewhere,

but I couldn't quite remember where. Belle reminded me.   "Joshua. The one in that note we found in the mansion. It said that he and the Old Man were waiting at Thornridge, obviously outdated information. I think it was signed by a fella named Butch or something."

"Interesting," I began conniving. "He can be quite useful to question." I turned to the guard who still had his gun on me, "Well partner, here's the way I see it. You're gonna lead me to this Joshua fellow, and in return, we are not going to blow your fucking face off. Do we have a deal?" The fifteen men behind me all drew their guns.

"Yes, sir, we do. Follow me." He put his gun down and led me to the Calico Hotel Joshua had taken as his headquarters. Walking into the hotel, something happened I was not exactly expecting.

"Mr. Clayton? Is that you?" the young gentleman at a large mahogany table asked, presumably Joshua.

"Yes. Do we know each other?" I was genuinely confused.

"Cold Harbor in '64. I was the kid from the 27th North Carolina. We were stationed just east of you. First North Carolina Cavalry, right? We traded coffee, remember?"

"Yes, you're one of Wilkins boys. I was sorry to hear of his passing at Petersburg. Of course, I remember you. What the hell happened?"

"I was picked up by a Federal who took me under his wing. He was killed, and I ended up moving west with nothing to my name. I was adopted by Elijah Calico, who raised me for a few years. Now I run his operations on this side of the valley. Now, enough about me, what the hell are you doing here?" We stared blankly at each other while I registered precisely what the hell just happened. "I uh- I'm here to talk about a business arrangement. Can we get the room?" I asked as I formulated something of a plan.

"Yes, of course. Clear it out, fellas. Mr. Clayton, have a seat."

"Yes, thank you. May I ask, have you heard about any of my exploits out here?"

"No, sir, I have not. Should I have?"

"Not necessarily. That being said, I do have important business with Elijah. It's regarding one of his trains-"

"Yes. The one that was tragically destroyed outside of Plainlanding." He looked through some papers. "$13,472.98 in damages." He paused and I was in utter disbelief.

"So you truly don't know why I'm here?"

"Can't say I do, sir."

"How old are you now, anyway?"

"18, sir. What is this about?"

"Well, you are an adult, I don't have to feel bad." I pulled out my colt and shot him in the face.

"You took mine, I'll take yours," I said to myself, walking out the door to the hotel, shooting the Calico goons. The rest of the posse did the same. Belle rode up to me with my horse and asked,

"What was that?"

"Just took care of an old friend and one of Elijah Calico's adoptive children. Time to move on to the next town."

The scene we left was a bloodbath. I even told the men to torch the hotel. Citizens of Boone came out of their hiding and started cheering. A few of them hopped on horses and joined us, too. It was as if we had just liberated the town from an evil tyranny. This was the desired effect of my exploits.

CHAPTER SEVENTEEN

◆ ◆ ◆

The next day, we made our way into the bustling city of Malvern, Texas. Our posse, now twenty-three strong, and now recorded in the roster thanks to Belle, was fixing for some rest and relaxation. Malvern was perfect. It was full of drunks, women, and everyone hated the Calico menace. The perfect place for the men to relax and for us to recruit more. So, we did our usual routine. We went into the biggest saloon, set up a table, bought a round of drinks, and began filling up our roster. Our quota was fifty for the trip, and we ended up with well over seventy after this. We stayed the night and moved on to the next town, repeating this process for a few days as we were in friendlier territory, not fifty miles from the border with New Mexico. And so, after a few days of successful recruiting, and a day or so of traveling, we made it back to Dallas with an unbelievable one-hundred-thirty-two people in tow. We told them to stay just outside the city as Belle and I went into the Dallas Railway station to meet Wolf, Hank, and Howie.

"Well, fellas, how'd we make out?" I asked.

"We got fifty." Howie replied. Hank handed me the roster, which I handed to Belle. Wolf, again, just gave me the menacing glare which signaled he, in fact, did not have a roster.

"That's good. How about you, Wolf?" He said nothing and merely gestured towards the ridge behind us, revealing dozens of Comanche Warriors.

"Yeah, that'll do it."

"How many did you get?" Hank asked.

"One hundred thirty-two." I replied, with confidence.

"Jesus. Didn't you only want a few dozen?" Hank stammered, "I guess Calico made a lot of enemies."

"Yes, sir, he did. Alright, fellas. Let's stop wasting time and take that gold mine. I'm sick of those bastards."

"You got it," Howie replied, walking back to their party.

Belle and I returned to our group and explained to them what was going to happen. They didn't even give us a chance to finish before cheering. So, with that, we took all of them around the outskirts of town, rendezvoused with Wolf, Hank, and Howie, and made our way to the mine, brute force being the order of the day. Over two-hundred-fifty Calico-hating fighters were storming his most profitable mine in these parts. The huge opening to the mine had two rails leading in and out. There were several carts of TNT that the men were using as weapons and for fun. From afar, it looked and sounded like a huge battle was raging inside that mine. It appeared as if a boot were stomping an ant hill. Gunshots, gun smoke, explosions, war cries and screams rattled the valley just outside the mine, not quite making it to the distant downtown Dallas. It was a hell of a sight. Wolf, Belle, Hank, Howie, and I never even went into the mine. We sat back, and watched as our huge swarm of men overtook the few guards defending the gold. Most of them were in and were funneling out mine cars filled with gold. Several cars filled to the brim with the purest gold in Texas. It was well over a ton of gold. Most of them came out, revealing the dirty work they had done in the mine. Some were covered in blood, others with dirt, most with the glimmering shine of gold. We were sitting on the ridge, adjacent to the mine. When the gunshots and explosions finally came to a stop, we came down to celebrate and congratulate our victorious band.

It was a hell of a sight to see. For all my time,

whether it be in the war, or out west, I had never seen such diverse groups of people uniting for a common cause. We had a huge band of Comanche, white veterans, black veterans, white farmers, black farmers, Mexicans, and Orientals. There was no hate, there was no discrimination, for all of these people shared one common goal. To bring down a harsh menace and a symbol of tyranny.

Suffice it to say, we had enough men to actually make a difference out here, and it did not change our goal. We were going to bring down the Calicos. Only, instead of one man at a time, we could do it one train at a time, or one town at a time. And so, with enough gold to keep these people on payroll, it was time to strategize.

"Alright fellas, listen up," I said to Hank, Wolf, Belle, and Howie, "This is what we're going to do. In order to maximize effectiveness, this is how we're going to keep it: Wolf, you take your warriors and wreak havoc in the countryside. Take down his wagon trains and liberate his farmers." He nodded. "Hank and Howie, we're going to pool our guys and split them in half. We should have about a hundred or so per. What you're going to do is liberate towns that he controls. Go town to town, torch his establishments, and free the townspeople stuck working under him." They rejoiced.

"Hell yeah!" Hank yelled.

"Belle and I, we're going after his trains. I think, with our small army, we can finally bring this asshole down, after all this time and all this destruction. I am proud of what we created. The Pierce Clayton Gang is now a formidable foe. I thank you all. Now, see to it that your men are paid, and set off. In one month, we meet back at the burned ranch in Amberwater. By then, the Old Man should have revealed himself, and will make a last stand to save whatever ass he has left." I took a deep breath after that long speech.

"Pierce. You're a god-damn hero," Hank said, giving me a bear hug. "You have no idea what it means to me and all of us. We all needed this vengeance."

"Of course. Now, will you please put me down?" I said, still firmly in his grasp.

"Oh yeah, sorry." He set me down, gently.

"I will see you at the old ranch. Good luck." Wolf took his party and set off into the sunset. Hank and Howie shook my hand, and also set off. Belle turned to me.

"You know, I'm really starting to like you."

She took off my hat.

"What do you mean, 'Starting'? Didn't you before-"

"Shut up." She reached up and kissed me. "Now, don't you have some army to lead or something?"

"This is more important." We shared another kiss as the sun set, the breeze rustling the surrounding bushes, and the delicate moonlight began illuminating the sky.

And so, one of the now biggest gangs in Texas split up, and began to wage war on the tyrannical Calico Gang. Only now, we had the numbers.

CHAPTER EIGHTEEN

◆ ◆ ◆

<u>One Month Later, Somewhere in North Texas</u>

"Hyah! Hyah!" I shouted while riding my horse alongside one of Calico's silver trains. A swarm of fellow gang members rode alongside, taking shots at the guards on the train. I emptied the cylinder of my colt and holstered it. Just as I had done several times before, I lifted out of my saddlebag and jumped onto the flat car of the train. A half dozen or so of my gang came with me. They walked behind me as I led the way through the train, reloading my trusty colt while bodies of guards and gangsters fell around me, thanks to the posse behind me and riding alongside. Gun smoke had completely filled the next car, and blood was splattered on the door leading in. So, I cocked my gun, opened the door and pointed the gun at the other end of the car. To my surprise, nothing in the car was visible. I walked very slowly, taking each step with caution, through the car until I came across a familiar face on the other side pointing a gun at me.

"Only one person alive has that gun." I said

as I grabbed Belle by the hips and kissed her. She jumped on the other side of the car, and we carried on through the train until we came across another locked car, only this one was armored and most likely harboring a few of Calico's brass. We moved up to the door, with plenty of guns behind us, and broke the lock. I kicked the door open and yelled,

"Don't move!" Men piled in behind me, pointing their guns at the two guards and the gentleman at a lavish desk. I holstered my gun and walked up to the fella.

"I presume you're Butch?" I looked him in the eye as he spit in my face.

"Ok." I said, wiping the spit and signaling my men to take him away.

"He's gonna come after you, Pierce! He's gonna come after you with an army! You won't be able to stop him!" He began hysterically laughing, as men dragged him to the back of the train and hogtied him. I sent a few more men to the front to take care of the rest of the guards and stop the train. Belle and I began to search Butch's private car. We found mostly reports from our previous raids, but most importantly, after busting open his locked desk, we found his personal correspondence with Elijah Calico. It read:

Butch-

I am growing sick and tired of Pierce Clayton and his goons. You have been completely ineffective in stopping his pillaging, and now I am forced to wire an old friend, which I did not want to do. I will bring a large force to Amberwater. Make yourself useful and draw them there, and for god's sake don't get yourself killed.
E. C.

Almost immediately after I finished reading that letter, a gunshot was heard from the back of the train, presumably one aimed for Butch. Nevertheless, the train was now at a complete stop, ripe for picking, and we finally knew, after weeks of pillaging, where to find and finish the Old Man. And now, we had the element of surprise. It was time to get the gang back together, and destroy this menace and whatever "old friend" he has to help.

CHAPTER NINETEEN

◆ ◆ ◆

A few weeks before, we had set up a large encampment in the woods near Amberwater. It had capacity for the entire gang of two-hundred-fifty, and was well protected by natural barriers. The perfect place for a camp and a base of operations. I sent runners to get word out to Wolf, Hank, and Howie to meet back at base camp for a meeting. After a day or so, we all met up at base.

"Fellas, it's great to see you." I said to the three of them as they walked into my tent. Belle was sitting to my left at a table.

"Likewise, Pierce. The stories of your exploits have been heard far and wide. A half dozen of Calico's trains you robbed. Is that right?" Hank asked.

"Yes sir. And the same goes for you, friend. You and Howie liberated thirteen towns and burned a devastating amount of his commercial operations." I turned to Wolf, "and you. You and your brothers have completed incapacitated his supply lines and devastated his wagon trains. We've all done great work. He will never be able to recover from this."

Howie chimed in. "Yes, sir. That is why we do it."

"I'm surprised he hasn't croaked from old age yet," Hank added.

"Well, he isn't dead yet, and that's why I asked to meet with all of you. We finally got him to show himself. He intends to trap us in Amberwater. He is bringing in a friend of his who he thinks will help him destroy us. I don't plan on letting that happen."

"This is perfect." Howie was jubilant, "This is exactly what we wanted."

"Yes it is. Have your men ready by dawn. The whole gang, whoever is battle ready, is riding for Amberwater. We will meet him head on."

"Ok.," Hank said, as he and Howie left the tent to tell their men. Wolf stayed behind.

"I want to take my warriors to the wood line. That is where we fight," he said bluntly and without moving more than his mouth.

"Yeah, do that. Whatever you think will work," I said, and he left without saying another word.

"That man is shrouded in mystery," I said to Belle.

"I think he likes you," she replied with a clever

grin.

I sat at my desk and began strategizing. We began preparing for the massive battle that lies ahead. The moment I had waited years for and what we had been working hard for. We had sacrificed so much for the greater good, and it was time to make sure, once and for all, that our lost and dead were avenged.

CHAPTER TWENTY

◆ ◆ ◆

The sun rose slowly and cast light through the trees, rendering the ground a pattern of light and dark. I had on my classic outfit. My old hat from the war, coat, vest, gold accouterments, cavalry boots, and my colt strapped to my hip. My Henry rifle was in Tanner's new black leather saddle. Belle was already packing the cylinders of her pair of golden revolvers. Men were tending to their horses outside and preparing themselves. Wolf had already set off with his raiders, and Hank and Howie were also ready to go at a moment's notice. And so, as the sun crept higher in the sky, we set off for Amberwater, a mere ten-minute ride out of the woods.

Belle, Hank, Howie and I led the Clayton Gang to battle. Two hundred men, with fifty Comanche as a surprise element, were the result of months of hard work, and it was finally time to destroy the heart of all evil: Elijah Calico. That was when we saw him, through my old field glasses, atop his old warhorse from the Mexican-American war. The damn thing was almost as old as he was. And next to him was the famed General Philip Sheridan. We fought him and his cavalry all throughout the war, and now he was commanding the army in these parts. He had been suppressing natives all over the region, from the Canadian border to the Mexican Border. As it would turn out, Elijah Calico's friend was a General with two-thousand men in addition to Calico's force, which numbered around three-hundred. I turned to Belle, Hank, and Howie.

"We've arrived at a crossroads." I took a deep breath. "We have two options: Turn and fight another day, and survive, or we fight now, and die trying." They said nothing. They only gave me the knowing glance. They wanted to make a last stand, and fight. So, Belle, Hank, and I traveled down to the town center, near the saloon which still had a busted window, to meet with General Sheridan and Elijah Calico in person. The swarm of Federal infantry and Cavalry had turned the outskirts of town blue, and the glint of their bayonets were blinding.

"Elijah Calico. General Sheridan," I said to them bluntly.

"You have been a very annoying thorn in my side, Mr. Clayton." That was all the Old Man had to say to me. General Sheridan piped up on his behalf.

"You have committed countless felonies

in your operations against Mr. Calico, including murder, arson, kidnapping, robbery, and more. You have cost the Federal government hundreds of thousands of dollars in damages, and are currently wanted by the State of Texas."

I never looked at the General, only stared at Calico.

"If you think for a minute I'm going to leave here with you alive and me dead, you are wrong. I will fight you until your pathetic empire is reduced to nothing but steel and bone." There was nothing but silence. We turned around and headed for the treeline, where the rest of the gang was waiting. From the treeline, we could see the Federal Infantry forming lines and the cavalry preparing to charge.

We waited for them to attack first, and luckily enough, they did. All the gang was mounted except for the Comanche, who moved in front of us and formed a spear wall. We advanced slowly forward as the Federal cavalry was charging full gallop at us. Five hundred of the best cavalry in the modern world were hurling themselves at us and about to hit the spear wall. The hooves kicking up dust and pounding the ground, hundreds at a time as if they were drums of war, inching closer and closer. When they hit the spear wall, their horses collapsed to the ground, and the men atop them were being shot by the rest of the gang. It was a massacre. A few dozen horses lay on the ground, and blue uniforms covered them. The remaining cavalry fell back in humiliated defeat. We had killed six dozen cavalrymen.

Their infantry had moved into the buildings of Amberwater, waiting for us to advance. Wolf came up to me and pointed to the treeline on the other side of Amberwater in the direction of the Comanche village. There I saw Chief Buffalo and his Comanche warriors waiting. There were hundreds of them, in addition to our two-hundred-fifty, now five-hundred strong. Wolf gave him a signal, and they launched fire arrows into the town's wooden buildings. They reduced them to smoldering embers with extreme speed and prejudice and, in combination with the scorching sun, the town had succumbed to ash. Hundreds of Federals burned alive or suffocated in smoke, and the rest went running.

I turned and shouted to the men, "Charge and cut them down! Bring me the Old Man!" The horsemen charged in first, guns in hand and filling the air with gun smoke, mixing with the black smoke from the fire. A hundred Comanche archers sat in the treeline launching arrows at the Federals who had attempted to form defensive lines. The other Comanche charged in with their guns and spears. General Sheridan was no longer present on the field, as he had retreated with a few dozen of his staff to the hills beyond Amberwater. The rest of the men in town were cut down. They were panicky, disorganized, and being destroyed in droves. Eventually, after brutal fighting, they too, fell back to the hills, reduced to only a few hundred. The Old Man's gang was almost completely destroyed as well. He was on the ground next to his horse, which had collapsed from heat exhaustion due to its old age. I rode over to him, dismounted, and stood over him. Wolf, Belle, Hank, and Howie joined me. We all took out our guns.

"My wife and daughter." Hank shot him in the leg. The Old Man screamed in pain and agony and began writhing on the ground.

"My people." Wolf shot him in his other leg as the screaming and crying grew louder.

"My brother." Howie shot him in the arm, and his fussing just continued.

"My husband." Belle shot him in the other arm.

"My wife and son. And everybody else you wronged." I fired a shot at the ground to heat up the barrel and put the end on his forehead. He began begging for mercy, almost completely crippled and hopeless.

"History will never forget what an evil soul it had on its hands. I'll see you in the world below us." I put a bullet in his forehead and the field fell silent for a few seconds. The puddle of blood coming out of the Old Man was the only thing audible for a time.

Then, the cheers. They were the loudest I had ever heard. Only a few dozen men were lost at this battle. But this was just the beginning. None of us could live normal lives after this. We were all wanted, and I was the kingpin of the biggest and most powerful gang in Texas. I wasn't the type to go into hiding, so I did what I knew best. I decided shortly after the Battle of Amberwater to wrong bad people who wronged good people. We would only steal from thieves and kill those who killed.

"I can't believe we did it." Belle said to us.

"It's about damn time."

And so, after all this time, the Calico menace was brought down. The Old Man and the rest of his gang were gone for good. We set out to achieve our goal, and we did it. The cost was high, but it was well worth the adventure.

EPILOGUE

◆ ◆ ◆

We carried on normal gang operations for a year before fading away. Hank and Howie would stay in the gang until their respective deaths. Howie died of Tuberculosis in 1871 and Hank was killed by a rival gang in New Mexico in 1873. Wolf would carry on liberating fellow Comanche all over the state of Texas and Oklahoma before passing away from natural causes at the ripe age of ninety-seven. Belle and I would get married in 1870 before rebuilding my old ranch just outside Amberwater. We would have two children, Henry and Leonard.

After Hank was killed, the gang dissipated. People left as we grew older and faded into obscurity, giving us the opportunity to be a happy family, without fame or danger of being killed. Amberwater was later rebuilt, and the Calico name would soon be forgotten. The Comanche experienced a brief period of prosperity until native conflicts with the Federal government ramped up.

Our children grew up happy and healthy. Henry went on to become a lawyer and later a state senator for Texas. Leonard would grow to join the military as a sailor and fight in the Spanish-American War.

This tale, as it is written, summarizes a period in my life that I was uncertain whether I was proud of or not. I started as an honest, hardworking farmer, and ended as a brutal criminal overlord of one of the most notorious gangs in the west. I came to realize that I had done the people a service. The Calico family was truly brutal and despicable. And, after telling this story, a story of this wild adventure, I was proud to have destroyed a true evil and reduced it to nothing but steel and bone.

Belle passed away in 1899 from pneumonia, and I would live through the first world war before passing away from unknown causes in 1922. My tombstone remains unmarked.

BOOKS BY THIS AUTHOR

High Horse

The compelling tale of an aspiring young officer that faces some of the most consequential decision making and events in United States History.

A Shot In The Dark

An intense insight into the wartime life of an old-fashioned artillery officer, who must learn the complexities of modern warfare during the American Civil War.

The Ultimate Resolution

A symbolic, literary representation of some of the most intense moments during the First World War told through the lense of the United States Marine 'Devil Dogs' and 'The Lost Battalion'.

1864

A battle-hardened veteran struggles with lingering traumatic effects after years of combat during the bloodiest conflict in the history of the United States.

After two years of brutal combat, he comes across
a young boy in the enemy trenches who knows
nothing of war and wants nothing to do with it,
and they must learn to adapt to one another, and
eventually learn to live without one another.

www.ingramcontent.com/pod-product-compliance
Lightning Source LLC
Chambersburg PA
CBHW020743160726

47993CB00006B/2589